YOUR MIXTAPE UNRAVELS MY HEART

Máire T. Robinson

Doire Press

First published in August, 2013.

Doire Press
Aille, Inverin
Co. Galway
www.doirepress.com

Editing: Sarah Moore
Cover image and design: Celina Lucey
Layout: Lisa Frank
Author photo: John Murphy

Printed by Clódóirí CL
Casla, Co. na Gaillimhe

ISBN 978-1-907682-24-7

Publication of *Your Mixtape Unravels My Heart* is the prize awarded Máire T. Robinson for winning the 2013 Doire Press International Fiction Chapbook Competition.

CONTENTS

Side A

Side B

To John Murphy and Catherine Robinson

SHIP OUT ON THE SEA

Sure any eejit could tell you that to win the Tidy Towns Contest you need to get yourself a boat, fill it with geraniums, and moor it beneath the town's welcome sign. Old water pumps are good too. They hint at the history of the place when *cailíní* in long skirts lined up with tin pails, before the water got contaminated with effluent or fertilizer run-off, or the well dried up altogether.

It's a strange reward for a town — not the most beautiful, not the biggest, not containing the most impressive architecture or decorous residents — but tidy, clean, manicured. Our town never did win that contest. Were you and I the reason why? The rogue elements on that wrought iron bench beside the boat. Two teenage girls chain-smoking, stomping about in heavy boots, observing it all from behind dark eyes: miscreant weeds that had taken root.

Do you remember that night we emancipated the boat? They'd never have believed we could shoulder that weight, but we did. And as we carried it down the narrow path to the sea, reeds bowed in greeting and the hawthorn blushed. The moon was shining just for us, illuminating a course across the dark sea. As we reached the water's edge, you turned to me and let out a whoop and your hair whipped about your head. We waded out and didn't care that our jeans got soaked. It was worth it to feel that boat cast off from our hands, to watch it set sail. We sat on the sand, smoking cigarettes until its outline was swallowed by the black horizon. But the next day, there it was, back under the welcome sign. No mark of the journey it had been on, apart from one tiny periwinkle shell stuck to its hull. We thought we'd done enough, but we were wrong. We should have captained that boat ourselves. That was our mistake.

I sat on the bench that day with fists clenched and talked about getting away from this place. You shook your head and told me that it's impossible to be in the middle of nowhere. Every place is home to someone, so you are always in the middle of somewhere. I had never thought of it that way, but then you were always saying things like that: stupidly profound or profoundly stupid—I could never figure out which. And after all that, you were the one who left and I'm still here.

Sometimes we'd sit there for hours, talking about nothing much and blowing smoke rings into the air, and we'd see them teetering past, stumble-drunk after closing time with their brown paper bags and late night vinegar running down their arms and the lack of kindness everywhere. And the girls, panda-eyed and lonely, hitching their bravado to their short skirts, were telling themselves that this was living. We said we would never be them. But there was one boy who had kind eyes. His hair was the colour of the sand and his smile promised everything. I told you he wasn't like the rest, but you didn't want to hear it.

I have a little girl now. She stares out to sea the way you used to, and tells me the places she will go. I swore I wouldn't get stuck in this town. Even as my belly swelled and he sat with his arm around me, I was filling his ears with the places we would go when she arrived, the three of us. It was a beautiful song I was singing and I believed it too at the time. But this place is home. It is somewhere, and like you said, every place is home to someone.

I wonder if you can see the sea from where you are, and if it smells the same. They're entering the contest again this year. I see them out in their high-viz vests with their plastic bin bags and their brooms. Sometimes I think it's a terrible affliction to yearn for disorder and chaos amidst all this cleanliness. I wonder how anyone can hope to leave a mark when everyone keeps tidying everything away. That spot on the bench that was home to our scrawled initials has long been painted over.

The boat is still there. I passed it the other day and thought of you and I found myself laughing. I've travelled a bit since you left, not abroad, mostly to coastal towns that are much like this one — always to the edge, but never past it. It's not just this place. Those boats are in every town: vessels manned by daffodils on a static voyage to nowhere. I would like to gather them in a fleet, then captain a pirate ship — the Gráinne Mhaol head on me — and lead them to where you are. We could sit together for a time and blow smoke rings and talk about nothing much in particular.

I STARTED SOMETHING I COULDN'T FINISH

A memory: I'm sitting on the floor of my bedroom in the old house, my trigger finger poised over the stop button, taping a song onto yet another mixtape. You have to press record and play at the same time. I'm listening to Atlantic 252. They play the same songs over and over: *...once there was this... seventy-four, Seventy-five... cats in the cradle... all that she wants...* It's pure shite really, but I don't know any better at the time. I picture them out on the ocean somewhere. A pirate station on a pirate ship. All of these DJs with their Mid-Atlantic accents and terrible pun names. Dusty Roads and Rick O' Shea. I nearly have the whole song... And then the nasal twang interrupts — *That one goes out to Sharon and all the girls...* Fucksake! I hit the stop button. Rewind rewind rewind. Then it makes this spluttering noise, the grinding of gears. Ah, Christ no.

Eject:

If it unravels, sometimes you can save it if you're careful. You need to unwind the tape from the spools, remove it gently from the machine. Use a pencil and wind it back up into the cassette. Chances are it won't be the same though. It might crackle or skip during a song. You can tape over it, but it's still there underneath. Sometimes you're better off unwrapping a brand new blank tape. Fuck it, anyway. Start over and this time it'll be right.

Fast forward forward forward. Stop. Play:

Edel with her little jars all lined up on the dressing table. She's rubbing cream on her face. It's only early but she's off to bed already. She has creams she puts on at night and creams she puts on in the morning. One for her face, her body, her hands, and those bits of skin on the sides of her fingers I call *cunticles* to annoy her. How she doesn't slide off the bed, I don't know. It never bothered me at the start, but after you've lived with someone for a while, it's different. I don't know, the illusion is shattered or something. Like seeing how the magic trick is done.

'Can you get me a glass of water, Coley?' she says, still looking at herself in the mirror. She's always drinking water. Can't go anywhere without a plastic bottle. Says it's important to stay hydrated. I used to call her my secret mermaid, tell her if she didn't behave I'd throw her off Nimmo's pier and she could swim back to her underwater cave or wherever-the-fuck. She used to laugh at that at the start.

I don't know when it happened but something's changed. She keeps saying *we're not students any more, Coley.* Suddenly everything we eat, drink, wear, and do is wrong. It's like she's living two lives, our life together and her notion of the life we should be living. During the week she's all: *let's go for a walk on the prom* and *I'm off to yoga* and *I can't eat that, it's got carbs in it* and *I have to get up early, can you keep the fucking noise down, please?* Then Weekend Edel appears. She's knocking back wine, smoking my cigarettes, saying do you reckon we could get pills? Later she's moaning and talking dirty like we're in a porno, ripping off my clothes. Weekend Edel starts to disappear again on Sunday evening when we're moping on the sofa with hangovers and she's looking at the leftover Chinese food and going 'Jesus, what shite am I after eating?' and she starts up that same old song of *never again, we're not students any more, Coley...*

Fast forward forward forward. Stop. Play:

She's on the pill, so I wonder. Yeah, I admit I do wonder. She makes the same joke to all of our friends, 'We don't like the word *accident*. We're calling it a surprise.' Now there's a whole new batch of creams and oils and soaks. She seems happier. I tell her I'm happy too. I tell myself how happy I am as I'm freezing my arse off, smoking on the balcony. She tells me one of the girls in work got engaged.

'Isn't that great?' she says and she looks up at me with her big don't-leave-me eyes, and I nod and see it all mapped out for me.

Fast forward forward forward. Stop. Play:

The night that it happens I'm not with Edel. It's supposed to be a quiet couple of pints with Dáithí, but you know how these things go. My battery dies and I don't get the messages. We end up at this party full of art students. Everyone's wired and everyone's talking to everyone else, like we're all in on something. There's a girl and two guys playing rock, paper, scissors in the corner for hours. The girl shrieks every time she wins and every time she loses. We get talking to this girl, Leonore. She's half French. Dáithí, like a total mong, goes and asks her if she only shaves under one armpit.

'Never heard that one before,' she says.

She's with this gangly fucker called Buttons we think is her boyfriend at first, but it turns out they're just friends from the art college. There's some rambling story about why he's called Buttons that myself and Dáithí don't listen to. Dáithí's scanning the room with a big stupid grin, chain-smoking and chewing the face off himself. I'm looking at Leonore and I swear there's a light coming from her. At first I think it's shining on her from overhead, but it spills from her mouth when she smiles. And I want that light. I want to taste it. Buttons laughs at all of Dáithí's shit jokes. 'You guys are sound,' he keeps saying, punching us on the arm and saying, 'Good man', giving us his beers and passing us spliffs. Leonore's father is some famous artist. Buttons says his name like we should know who he is, so we just nod and go, 'Oh yeah? No way, man'.

Leonore's telling us about her artwork. 'Found art is a great excuse to pick stuff up off the street,' she smiles. She says she likes to reappropriate things she finds that are old or useless.

'You'll like Coley, so,' says Dáithí.

Buttons laughs and thumps him on the back. 'Good one!'

I want her to see that I'm not like Dáithí. 'That sounds amazing,' I goes. 'I'd love to see it.'

'You can come to our end of year exhibition,' she says. 'It's on in the college.'

She tells me she's just bought these tapes at a car boot sale. Most of them are blank but one has *Mixtape For Joe* written on it and it's decorated with love hearts. She wants to see what's on it but she has nowhere to play it.

'Tapes,' I goes. 'Fucking hell.' I haven't thought about them in so long and suddenly I'm there, sitting on the floor of the old house again listening to the radio. 'Here, Dáithí, do you remember tapes?'

'Jesus,' he goes. 'Tapes!' and then we're shaking our heads and we keep going *Tapes, Jesus, Tapes...* Buttons and Leonore are just looking at us and laughing.

'You fuckers are too young to have had tapes,' says Dáithí.

'I'll get you a tape recorder,' I says to Leonore. 'I'll sort you out. Don't worry.' It seems really important in this moment to promise her this. It seems really important to listen to that tape and see what's on it. Like nothing else matters.

Later, we do lines together in the bathroom and it just happens. Afterwards, she pulls up her knickers and saunters down the stairs and back to the party like it never happened. Later I look at her dancing, that light spilling around her and it seems impossible that it happened.

Rewind rewind rewind. Stop. Play:

It's like looking back at two people who aren't us. Like remembering this film I saw once. We're off on one of our road trips, me and Edel.

Neither of us can drive so we're on a bus, heading off to some town or other just for the day. I like the feeling of movement. Headed towards some place together, a destination. It doesn't matter where. Something always happens on the way. We spot something funny from the window that we can't stop laughing at, or we find ourselves remembering stories that we tell each other. It's at the start and we can't not touch. Every part of her is an invitation. Our mouths are opposing magnets. Travelling together through all of these towns that are best viewed in movement, never stopping. There's bypasses around most of them now.

Fast forward forward forward. Stop. Play:

I'm walking Leonore to the bus stop. We're standing on the footpath at the traffic lights.

'I play a game,' she says, 'when I'm waiting for the lights to change. I look at the people waiting on the other side and choose one I'd sleep with.'

'Why?'

'That's the game,' she says. 'It makes things more interesting. Otherwise you're just standing there waiting for that green light.'

'So you do this every time you cross the road?'

'Yeah.'

'What if it's all pensioners on the other side?' I goes.

'You still have to pick one.'

'What if it's all girls?'

'That wouldn't bother me.' she goes.

She looks at the people on the opposite side. She's really concentrating. She doesn't laugh or smile or anything. If this is a game, she's taking it very seriously.

'Him,' she says finally, nodding towards this bald fucker at the end of the line who looks like a geography teacher or something.

'That guy?' I say.

'He's got kind eyes,' she says.

'You can see his eyes from here?'

'You choose.'

I look along the line of people on the other side, but the lights change then. The green man appears and everyone streams across.

'You missed your chance.'

'Typical,' I say and put my arm around her as we cross the road.

Rewind rewind rewind. Stop. Play:

I crawl home the morning after the party, hangin'. Let myself in the door and I see Edel sitting there on the sofa with her sister, Phidelma. The sister never liked me for some reason, and now she's giving me daggers even more than usual. I try to take in what they're saying about the baby.

'You should have been there,' says Phidelma. 'I mean, we rang you from the hospital I don't know how many times. We left messages...'

'My phone...' I goes and I look at the floor.

'I think you should go,' says Edel and her voice is so small, but her eyes tell me she means it. 'Phidelma's gonna stay with me for a while.'

This is the scene that replays. There's no erasing it because it happened. I just stand there. I don't say anything. I just nod and then I leave.

So I head over to Dáithí's. I'm still scagged out of it and nothing seems real. I keep thinking, I'll just sleep and when I wake up I'll figure everything out. I'll make it right. I pass some auld lad giving out flyers at the entrance to the university.

'Do you believe in life after death?' he says and holds one out to me. I glare at him and I want to tell him how fucking shit his timing is, but I find myself reaching out to take the leaflet. I ball it up in my pocket as I walk past the cathedral. By the time I'm on Francis Street I think of what I should have said to him: *No, I believe in death after life.* As I'm passing Cash Converters, I see the tape recorder in the window.

Fast forward forward forward. Stop. Play:

Leonore calls over to Dáithí's place. In the daylight with no makeup on she looks younger. I bring her upstairs and roll a spliff as she gets the tape from her bag and puts it in the deck. She presses play. It splutters, then makes that grinding noise where you know the whole thing is fucked.

'Shit,' I say. 'Hang on, maybe we can save it.' I look around for a pencil. She presses eject and tries to pull the tape out.

'It broke,' she goes. For a second I think she might cry.

'Shit. This is probably why they invented CDs.'

She laughs then. 'Maybe I can still use it for my mural.' She starts pulling the rest of the tape out of the cassette, winding it around her fingers.

'Poor Joe,' she goes. 'We'll never know what was on his tape now.'

She sits beside me on the bed and we smoke the spliff.

'I wouldn't feel bad for this Joe fella,' I goes. 'The tape ended up at a car boot sale, so he mustn't have given two fucks about it, in fairness like.'

'What if he never got it? Some girl made it for him but never gave it to him?'

I don't know what to say to that, so I put my arm around her and kiss her. We fuck on top of the covers. She still has that piece of tape wrapped around her fingers.

Fast forward forward forward. Stop. Play:

I'm waiting for the lights to change so I can cross the road and I find myself looking at the faces on the opposite side the way Leonore did that time. At the end of the line of people, I see Edel with her new boyfriend. He has his arm around her and I don't know where to look. I've done well not to bump into her so far. Galway's small really when you think of it, but I heard she moved out to Headford so I suppose she's not around as much. They bought a house out there after they got engaged. I used to think I'd like to have a drink with her. Just talk. But I don't know. Maybe that's stupid. What good is that to anyone now? She sees me then and she raises her hand. I wave back. She gives me that uncertain smile she used to give me at the start, with one corner of her mouth. The lights change. We cross to opposite sides of the road and we both keep walking.

Rewind rewind rewind. Stop. Play:

'Here, can you just take this wine?' Dáithí grabs two glasses and knocks one back. I go to take one off him. 'Get your own,' he says, laughing as he starts drinking the second one.

The exhibition is in the art college. You have to walk through a series of connected studios to see everything. The walls are tall and white and there's all sorts of stuff on display: paintings, video pieces, little ceramic pots and shit.

'I'm gonna go find Leonore,' I say to Dáithí's back as he wanders off into a room filled with black and white photos of nudes.

'Sound,' he says without looking back.

It makes sense when I see her mural. It takes up a whole wall. Spirals of unravelled tapes, waves of sounds. Mixtape For Joe is at the centre of it all. And it's sad. All those hormones raging, love sickness contained in three minutes, twenty seconds. All those la las, and yeah, yeahs that meant something to someone at the time. No one is listening to them now. She's surrounded by people. Everyone wants to talk to her, to congratulate her. I make my way though the crowd and she kisses me on the cheek, thanks me for coming.

'We'll catch up later,' she says. 'There's just someone I need to speak to.'

'Sure,' I goes. 'I'll have a look around.'

She's swallowed up by the crowd and I don't see her for the rest of the evening. We look for her as we're going to leave, but she's already left.

Fast forward forward forward. Stop. Play:

Her phone rings out. I leave messages. I text her. Then it doesn't ring at all. I see Buttons around town but he just shrugs and smiles his stoned smile.

'I heard she went to Amsterdam. Some scholarship,' he says.

I never washed the sheets and I search them inch by inch for any trace of her smell, the tang of her. I keep seeing her walking out to the bathroom that last time without a stitch on her. A part of me wants to make her ashamed, to watch her cringe and cover herself up.

'Fucksake, are you not cold?' But she just throws back her head and laughs. You don't like it, too bad, the laugh says. I really couldn't give a flying fuck, the laugh says. And maybe she scared me a little.

Forward forward forward. Stop. Play:

I'm crossing the road and I find myself looking at the faces on the other side. I don't take them in. I look away, try to think of something else, but I can always see her there with him. I fix my attention on that red light and I don't look at anyone.

Forward forward forward... *Turn green, you fucker. Turn Green.*

THE MOON ASKED THE CROW

Once Declan made the decision, he found it easy to become a bird-watcher. It wasn't like golf where you had to learn the rules, join a club, and wear diamond-patterned socks. He simply bought a pair of binoculars, a notebook, a pen, and a copy of *Bird-Watching in Ireland*. He could amble along now, alone, but with a sense of purpose. Not happy exactly, but occupied.

They were everywhere. If you listened you could hear them over the noise of the workman's drilling, the school children's bullying, the boy racers' beeping. They wailed like newborns, screamed like vengeful spirits, swam with the shit and the beer cans in the canal. They roosted on rooftops, scavenging rubbish, eating scraps. Now that he could identify the birds, he noticed them even more. There were wagtail and dipper in the River Corrib and in the canals. There were heron and kingfisher in Lough Atalia. In late April and early May, you could see whimbrel on Mutton Island, enjoying their annual trip to the sewage treatment plant. The best time of all though was winter.

Declan no longer dreaded winter. It no longer meant Christmas

Day alone and Helen's annual call, her voice full of pity and contempt. His son being put on the phone and told to 'thank daddy' for this year's unwanted present. Now, winter meant standing on Nimmo's Pier spotting the gulls. Not just any old gulls. Rare gulls. Special gulls that bird-watchers from all over the world flocked to see.

Ross's Gull (Rhodostethia rosea)
Named after the North Pole explorer, James Clark Ross, it is the only species in its genus. Identification:
- *Small pale grey and white gull with wedge-shaped tail.*
- *Distinctive black collar around the neck.*
- *Similar in plumage to the Little Gull (Hydrocoloeus minutus) but larger and longer winged.*

When Declan was six, he found an injured bird cowering in the corner of the garden. At the time he thought it was a blackbird, but looking back on it now, it was probably a baby rook. It had been attacked by something, the neighbours' fat tomcat most likely. The bird beat its wings pathetically, but could not fly. It emitted startled squawks. Declan scooped it up in an empty cardboard box and brought it into the kitchen. His father looked at it and shook his head. He took the tiny creature up into his hands.

'For its own good,' he said to Declan. He placed his fingers around the bird's neck and there was a sharp snapping sound like a dry twig.

Declan took his notebook and biro from the inside pocket of his Parka.
NIMMO'S PIER, Jan 8:
3 x American Herring Gull
4 x Ring-billed Gull

No Ross's Gull. There had been reports of sightings on birdwatchers' websites a couple of days ago. He would try again tomorrow. It was starting to rain as he put his notebook and pen back in his pocket and made his way down the pier. There was a lone dark-haired woman taking shelter under the Spanish Arch. She was wearing a crimson woolly hat and Declan noticed the binoculars around her neck. As he approached, she suddenly waved at him and beamed. There was a general camaraderie between bird-watchers. Recognition of their common pursuit was usually acknowledged with a smile or nod. The woman's familiarity with him made him stall. Did she know him? An old friend of Helen's maybe. But then, surely, she wouldn't be waving at him so cheerily.

'Here to see the gulls?' she called and he realised he didn't know her at all. She was just one of those people. She probably struck up conversations with strangers on trains.

Rook *(Corvus frugilegus)*
Identification:
- *A species of crow with all black plumage, which can show a red or purple sheen in certain light.*
- *Intelligent and social in nature.*
- *Similar in appearance to the Carrion Crow, but the rook has a more peeked crown.*

She asked him if he knew of a good spot for a bite to eat. 'Nothing fancy.' He said he knew just the place. He led her in the opposite direction from the Italian restaurants and eateries of Quay Street, like two salmon swimming upstream.

'I'm Gladys,' she smiled.

'Declan,' he said as he shook her hand. It was as fragile and white as one of Helen's china cups.

They crossed Wolf Tone Bridge and went to a place he knew on Dominick Street. Gladys smiled when she saw the linoleum floor, the faded floral PVC tablecloths, and the framed photograph of Pope John Paul II's visit to Ireland in 1979.

After Helen left him he had come here a lot. You got a decent feed and didn't have to pay an arm and a leg. Helen used to laugh and say that he only thought he'd eaten a proper dinner if it included potatoes. She tried to make him eat pasta and cous cous. At least he could eat what he wanted now. There was always a silver lining.

He looked at Gladys sitting opposite him. She had removed her heavy duffel coat and looked tiny, perched on her seat. She was wearing a black woollen jumper, a black skirt to the knee, thick black tights, and those furry boots women seemed to favour nowadays. She took off her rain-soaked red hat. The fluorescent light shone on her from overhead, making her hair glint with iridescent streaks of purple, like Indian ink. He wondered if she dyed it. His own hair had started turning grey when he was twenty-one. He decided that she was definitely younger than him, but not by much. If he had to guess, he'd say she was thirty-five. If she asked him to guess, he would tell her thirty. He rubbed his hand over his chin and thought to himself that he really must shave. He could feel the prickles of hair on his neck sticking into his black polo neck.

Gladys ordered the stew with a side portion of soda bread. Declan ordered the roast turkey dinner, with potatoes.

He smiled at her. 'For someone so small you've a big appetite.' Then he worried it was the wrong thing to say. Women could be funny about food, he knew that much, but she beamed.

'I'm starving! I've been standing on that pier all day.' Her voice didn't sound like it belonged to her. She looked like she should have the high-pitched voice of a tiny girl, but hers was a deep conspiratorial voice. Every sentence sounded like she was letting him in on a secret just between the two of them.

It would be rude not to invite her for a drink, thought Declan. She was from Wicklow and didn't know anyone in town. Otherwise she'd just be sitting there, bored, in her B&B on College Road. He brought her to Freeney's and they sat in the corner. The pub hadn't changed in donkeys' years and there was something reassuring about that. There must be a recommendation for it in some tourist book or other, something about 'the genuine Irish pub experience'. He often spotted rain-coated tourists surveying the bar and sipping Guinness tentatively. Gladys asked for a white wine which he felt showed a touch of class. Helen drank vodka, but then Helen drank anything. That was the problem, at least as he saw it.

Gladys told him she'd grown up near Kilcoole, where her father had taken her bird-watching at weekends. She'd learnt early on to recognise the different species: lapwing, brent, curlew. When most little girls were asking for teddy bears and Barbie dolls for their birthdays, Gladys was asking for binoculars and bird books. Declan thought of Seán, how he'd envisioned buying him his own pair of binoculars. In the early days he had big plans for Seán's monthly visits. These days there was always some excuse: a friend's birthday, a football match. When he did come to stay, Seán moved about Declan's house like a ghost. He spent his time playing computer games or cocooned by giant headphones.

Declan felt a lump in his throat. He coughed.

'Same again?' asked Gladys.

She asked him if he'd heard about the ravens in Britain. He shook his head.

'There's been reports of flocks attacking livestock,' she said. 'The farmers want their protected status lifted so they can shoot them.'

'That can't be right,' said Declan. 'It's carrion they eat, unless the animals were sick or dying.'

'No, the farmers said the animals were healthy. The ravens ate them alive. Pecked out their eyes. Ate their tongues and their underbellies.'

Declan wondered what it could mean. He found himself thinking of the little bird he had rescued as a boy, so tiny even in his small boyish hands, and that snapping sound that had stayed with him all these years, the cold finality of it. For a moment he thought he was about to tell Gladys. If he could find the right words, or even the right word to start off, it would all tumble out. He took a long swig of his pint.

As the lights flashed for last orders they were taking turns listing group names for birds. He presented her with a bouquet of pheasants. She accepted with a charm of finches. He offered her a murmuration of starlings. She gave him a tidings of magpies. It might have been his imagination, but it seemed she had moved closer to him. Her hand was resting on the table and he fought an urge to reach out and take it in his own.

He offered to walk her to her B&B but she said there was no need. He extended his hand and she shook it with a laugh. As he walked home, hands in pockets, he thought to himself that he should have kissed her on the cheek, or maybe even on both cheeks. That was what people did these days. Maybe then she would have turned her head and kissed him on the mouth.

As he let himself into the flat, he imagined Gladys was with him and he saw it through her eyes. He inhaled the musty dank smell of the place. There was a cold clamminess to the air that stuck to the skin like wet clothing. He saw the dirty cups and plates on the table, the pile of old newspapers on the chair, the take-away curry that had solidified in its container. He opened the window and cold, clean night air came flooding in. First thing tomorrow, he would get this place in order. *First thing.*

He looked out over the city. A soft rain was falling. It haloed the street lights and made the pavement shine glossy. He wanted to fly to where she was, over the rushing Corrib, past the shadowed cat stalking the terraced rooftops of Bowling Green. He would curl past the three clock faces of Saint Nicholas's Church and float over Shop Street and the last of the revellers traipsing home to lonely beds, or entwined with hopeful new loves, bolstering each other up as they stumbled like casualties of war along the slick streets. He would pass the tiny sliver of a crescent moon that lay discarded in the sky like a cut fingernail and rap on her bedroom window and they would swoop together over the city. He knew this was the way it would be. Something inside of him was unfurling. He was stretching, testing his wingspan. He would tell her things, or not tell her things, or just listen while she told him things. It was terrifying and it was good.

ANOTHER BREAKFAST WITH YOU

Love and hate are the same thing. I know that now. It's only the temperature that's different, like bread and toast, or cheddar and fondue. I would love if Malachy hated me; to know he lays awake at night fuming as my name reverberates in his head; that images of me flash into his mind unbidden, leaving scorch marks on his retina; that he shuffles about his house when nobody is home cursing me aloud to the sink, the table and chairs, the hardwood floor — *Fuckin' bitch... stupid fucking cunt* — that he tears out his black hair in clumpfuls from the sheer frustration of trying to contain his hatred of me. But he doesn't. I gave him no reason to. I know that now he feels nothing for me but the opposite of love, and the true opposite of love is not hate, but indifference.

After him, I was restless. I changed jobs. I changed hair colour. I changed city. After him, I was burned, cautious. I'd start seeing some fella and I'd worry he'd be just like Malachy. Then I'd end up disappointed when it turned out he wasn't. In Galway, I found work with a temp company like the one I'd worked for in Dublin. I got to know the outskirts of the city, the bus routes to the business parks, the different names of the endless roundabouts, the grey houses that lined the streets like crooked teeth. I answered phones and took messages and filed bits of paper, but it was different now. Before my days had been filled with him, like a drug: waiting to see him, then seeing him, then thinking about having seen him. Now there was this void. I wondered how people knew what they were supposed to do with their lives. I could see it there, my life playing out in front of me, but it was like this foreign thing I couldn't get inside.

I heard someone say once that the break-up of a relationship is like a death that only two people experience. So I suppose you could say that I mourned when it was over, but he didn't. I saw the pictures of his engagement party in *Irish Society Magazine*. He was beaming, indecently gleeful. *Food columnist, Hannah Richardson, celebrates her engagement to Dublin barrister Malachy McNulty.* In the interview she said when they had met and the dates didn't add up. In the photos, he was wearing the cornflower-blue shirt I gave him for his birthday. The one I couldn't afford, but bought anyway because I knew the colour would bring out his eyes. And it did.

When I was made redundant, it didn't bother me at first. I thought I'd find some other office work like I always had in the past. But every day of the week people were losing their jobs. Businesses were closing down. A Burger King opened in Galway and a thousand people showed up for the open job interviews. It made the evening news. All these architects and teachers and accountants desperate for work: kids to feed, mortgages to pay. At least I didn't have that to worry about. So, I sank into my unemployment like a relaxing bath. I wore pyjamas all day. I watched daytime TV. I drank. Sometimes I was filled with a giddy feeling of getting away with something, like when you'd be off sick from school and you could watch telly all day, and you'd laugh to yourself thinking of all the saps at their desks doing maths. But other times I was filled with fear, a paralysis that made leaving the flat impossible.

I was flicking channels one day, and there she was, Malachy's wife. *Home Cooking With Hannah.* She was wearing a floral apron and smiling at the camera as she sifted flour into a bowl. I realised that it wasn't some TV studio done up to look like a kitchen. It was their kitchen, in their farmhouse in County Wicklow. I recognised it from that magazine spread they did after their daughter was born. They were photographed in various rooms, all *restored faithfully using local materials.* I know I shouldn't have looked at it. I couldn't not look at it.

I could see why Hannah had been given her own TV show. She wasn't like those female chefs you see on British TV, food pornographers mugging for the cameras and describing everything as 'orgasmic'. She was natural and understated. I'd seen her photo before but never heard her voice. I liked the way her diction trilled with polished pronunciation. She sounded Irish, but not Irish. What you might call West-Brit if you felt like insulting her. Listening to her speak, you couldn't help but picture a childhood filled with pony rides, skiing trips, ballet recitals and various social engagements with the type of people who use 'summer' as a verb. The type of childhood Malachy also had, and now their children would have. I knew that *they* summered in Tuscany. She loved the bold rustic flavours of the region. She wrote about them in her first book, *Bold Rustic Flavours of Tuscany.*

I started watching Hannah's show every day. There was something reassuring about her, something indestructible. A toxic gas cloud could float over from Sellafield killing everything in its wake, making no allowances for school children or baby seals or high-ranking civil servants, and there she would be still baking scones in her Aga, an invisible force field of middle-class charm rendering her untouchable. After a few weeks, I even attempted some of the recipes. Sometimes she mentioned him and I imagined their life together.

'These freshly baked scones are just perfect for family get-togethers. They're a particular favourite of my husband's,' she said.

I used to cook breakfast for Malachy the odd time he stayed over.

'Don't you know how to cook anything other than eggs?' he said.

'Eggs are good for you. They contain protein.'

'So does steak.'

He never stuck around for long. Always work to do, or so he said, even at weekends. 'Your flat is always so fucking cold.'

'So come back to bed and I'll warm you up.'

'Be sure not to over-handle the dough as this can make the scones rubbery. Place them close together on the tray. This will encourage them to rise, not spread.' Hannah tapped the underside of the scones and they made a hollow sound. 'Perfect,' she said.

'Perfect,' I mimicked as I tipped out the burnt solid mass that hit the counter like a brick.

The day we found out our jobs were gone, everyone was talking on their phones, or crying, or crying into their phones. I felt stupid just standing there. I couldn't cry and I couldn't think of anyone to call so I rang the talking clock. *At the beep, the time will be 12.22. Beeeep.* Jim Fahy was at the gates with his RTE News microphone, asking people for their reactions.

'How are you feeling?' he asked me.

'Grand,' I said. I was thinking that he looked much taller than he does on telly. 'I mean, terrible. It's terrible. Sorry about that. I think I'm in shock.'

On the bus home I wondered what I'd look like on screen. Later, I watched the evening news but I hadn't made the cut. Instead, they used a clip of Gráinne from accounts. 'I don't know what I'm going to do!' she wailed into the camera lens. The light fell on her face, showing up the line of downy hair on her upper lip and the purplish shadows under her eyes that looked like bruises.

The more I watched Hannah's show, the more my cooking started to improve. I found myself getting up early, making shopping lists and scowering supermarket shelves for ingredients. I stopped spending my dole money on vodka and cigarettes and started buying things like pimento stuffed olives and vanilla pods. One day I went into town and enrolled on a cookery course. On my way home, I stopped into the newsagents. There was a picture of Malachy and Hannah on the front of one of the tabloids. 'TV Chef's Love-Rat Hubbie in Au Pair Shocker' screamed the headline. I skimmed through the article, then bought a copy and headed home to read it properly.

Inside the newspaper, there were pictures of the au pair alongside her 'exclusive story' of the affair. 'We liked to get steamy in the kitchen,' she was quoted as saying. Then at the end of the article alongside a photo of her staring mournfully into the middle-distance: 'I still have feelings for Malachy.' The strange thing is, she looked just like Hannah, only a less polished version, like some second-rate actress who had been hired to play Hannah in one of those 'straight to DVD' biopics. It was as if Malachy had thought he wanted the new, but the familiar won out, like going abroad but drinking in an Irish bar. Maybe she was an act of rebellion, an antidote to all that perfection.

Every day, there were more and more revelations in the papers. I read them over coffee in my tiny kitchen, which felt different now, warmer, transformed by the daily smell of fresh baking. More women came forward with stories of their affairs with Malachy. There was speculation that Hannah would leave him, that she would cancel her forthcoming book tour. Still, she refused to be interviewed and never made a statement. There she was on TV every day as always.

'Perfect,' she said as she piled the almond and orange zest moon-shaped biscuits onto a floral serving tray. And they were perfect. And so was she, the chaos of the universe controlled in her measured stirring of the eggs and the way she sifted the flour just so.

When I told Malachy I was pregnant, he offered me money, said he'd take care of everything. I told myself he would change his mind. I waited. I pictured the new life we would have together, the three of us. Maybe I pictured this new life as something like those photos of him and Hannah in *Irish Society Magazine*. But then I stopped waiting because there was nothing to wait for anymore.

'Maybe it's for the best,' he said. 'We had fun though, didn't we?' As if we'd been playing a game of pool and our hour was up. *Had.* Just like that.

I bought my copy of *Home Cooking With Hannah* and stood in line. I could see her smile and sign books for the people up ahead. I opened the book and looked inside. It was dedicated *To My Darling Husband, Malachy*. I edged forward in the line. I wanted to tell her that we were the same. I wanted to kick over her display of books and spit in her face. I wanted her to see that we were not the same. I wanted to ask her which of his faces he showed to her and which of his faces was real. I wanted to tell her how tired it made me, hating somebody because they didn't love me. I wanted to ask if she was tired too. I wanted to take her hand and lead her out into the street to run and run in the rain until we were both out of breath and laughing like in a film.

I remembered then the feeling I had when me and Malachy were together, like I could never get close enough to him. I used to scrape my fingernails down his back to make him bleed, to claim him, but it was no good. Even with my arms around his neck, my mouth on his, our bodies entwined, we were too far apart.

'I want to open you up and crawl inside,' I told him and he gave me his lazy smile like he understood what I meant. But I don't know anymore. When I picture it now, it looks more like a smirk. What I remember most is his mouth, and always the surprising coldness of his kiss.

At the top of the queue, Hannah smiled at me. 'Hi there, thanks for coming,' she said, reaching to take the book from my hands. 'Who will I make this out to?'

WE SHARE OUR MOTHERS' HEALTH

Daisuke woke before his alarm as usual. Although his curtains were open, morning had not yet broken and he switched on the light to get dressed. The smell of miso soup used to be his alarm call. Back then, he would follow it to the kitchen where his mother was already up and dressed, singing along with the radio while she prepared breakfast, the air heavy with warmth and the dark windows clouded over with condensation.

Easing the sliding door closed behind him, Daisuke crept out of his bedroom, taking care not to make too much noise for fear of waking his father in the next room. He could hear the old man's strained breathing, constant and raspy as wind through a gap in a sail, as he tiptoed through the kitchen. His mother used to prepare a lunch of rice balls and tea for Daisuke and his father to take with them on the boat. As they headed into the half-lit morning, they would turn to see her framed in the doorway. 'Ki o tsukete,' she would call. *Take care.*

These days, Daisuke waited until after work to eat, picking up bento boxes for himself and his father at the convenience store on his way home.

He used to bring fish, but recently if his father saw it, he shook his head like a stubborn child. 'It's bad.'

'No, it's fine now, Dad. That was a long time ago,' Daisuke would try to convince him. 'Look, it's mackerel, your favourite.' But the old man wouldn't budge. He wondered if inside his father's head it was a different year.

It started before Daisuke and his brother were born. Their parents told them that it began with the cats. They clawed at invisible tormentors, yowling and running in circles as their bodies jerked and twitched. Disorientated, they ran at walls or jumped into the sea. Birds fell from the sky and a blanket of dead fish covered Minamata bay. Next, the townspeople fell ill. Their hands and feet no longer obeyed them. The world became blurred and voices echoed in caves. Some looked at their parents, husbands, wives, or children and saw the smiling faces of strangers. Words lodged in their throats and choked them until they coughed up blood and their bodies convulsed. Babies were born with withered limbs and swollen brains and doctors couldn't say why. Some people couldn't control the nonsensical yells that escaped from their mouths and were committed to asylums. Others fell into a deep sleep, never to wake again. For years, nobody knew what caused the illness so they called it *neko odori byo* — cat dancing disease, but in time it came to be known as Minamata disease, after the town itself.

As Daisuke was heading for the front stoop to put on his wellington boots, he heard his father calling him.

'Dad?' he said, easing the sliding door open and peering into his father's room. 'Are you okay?'

'Hiroshi?' called the old man's voice in the dark.

'No, Dad. It's me, Daisuke.'

'Hiroshi?'

Daisuke sighed. 'Hiroshi is in Tokyo, Dad.'

His father blinked hard and looked at him. 'Ah, yes. Of course,' he said.

This was what he said these days if he was unsure about anything, the affirmative expression at odds with the look of confusion on his face.

'Can I get you something?' asked Daisuke.

His father sat up, frowned, then reached for the glass of water beside his futon. He raised it to his mouth where it danced in front of his lips.

Daisuke stepped towards him. 'Can I help?'

His father batted the offer away with his free hand. Daisuke watched as he drank some water and placed the glass back down in a shaky arc.

'I have to go, Dad, but I'll be back soon and I'll bring you something to eat. Okay?'

His father nodded, then his face lit up all of a sudden. 'Cigarettes!' he said, pointing a triumphant finger at Daisuke. 'Don't forget my cigarettes.'

'Okay, Dad,' he said as his father placed his head back on the pillow.

Takeshi was already sitting on the low wall beside the dock when Daisuke approached. He had hired Takeshi to help out when his father finally retired, when sheer pride was no longer enough to provide him with the physical strength he needed to sustain him through the gruelling hours on the boat. Daisuke was unsure about hiring Takeshi at first.

He had approached Daisuke on the dock, shoulders hunched, a cigarette dangling from his lip as he nodded towards the boat. 'I hear you're looking for someone.'

Daisuke looked him over. He couldn't be more than twenty, this lanky kid with scrawny arms and dyed-blonde hair that stood at impossible angles even in the wind. He couldn't imagine him working on a boat. He looked like one of those punks who worked in a games arcade or pachinko parlour. There was something familiar about him that Daisuke couldn't place. It was only later that he realised Takeshi reminded him of his brother Hiroshi before he moved to Tokyo for university, back when Hiroshi was the old Hiroshi.

'It's hard work,' Daisuke said, 'early starts.'

Takeshi shrugged, 'That's fine.'

'It's windy out there, you know? You might ruin your hair.'

'I'll wear a hat,' said Takeshi.

The two men faced each other with stony expressions, neither one backing down.

Daisuke sighed, 'Okay, if you're really serious about this you can come out with me tomorrow.'

He was convinced the kid wouldn't show, but there he was the next morning, and every morning since, sitting on the low wall waiting for Daisuke, the peak of his Fukuoka Hawks baseball cap pulled low over his face.

'Ohayo!' he called to Takeshi, as he sat beside him and lit a cigarette.

Takeshi acknowledged Daisuke with his customary nod as he continued to smoke. This had become a morning ritual for the men: looking out to sea and inhaling the sweet tobacco, readying themselves for the day's work. Then, as though some invisible signal had passed between them, they stood in unison and boarded the boat.

The water was calm and dark as they cast off. Heading out to sea, the silence was broken by a lone gull that swooped low and screeched. When they reached the spotter boat off the coast, the sun was starting to come up. Looking back toward shore, Minamata resembled a sleepy village in a painting yet to come to life. Small wooden houses were dotted in front of hills covered in rich, green trees. Dominating the skyline was the metallic factory at the edge of the bay.

When the people of the town began to get sick there were whispers among Daisuke's father and the other fishermen that the chemical factory could be the cause. The fish were dying so there must be something in the water, and the factory pumped its wastewater into the bay, but the factory had brought prosperity to the town and almost half the townspeople worked there. Such a thing was unthinkable.

Daisuke turned the gauge to release the net and the old sea-worn ropes creaked as they were unravelled from the spool and dropped into the sea. It was the job his father used to do, and it still felt strange to be the one doing it. They trawled with the net stretched out between theirs and the spotter boat. It became choppier as they headed further out. Green waves speckled with white foam danced around them. Daisuke and Takeshi put on their raincoats to protect them from the salt water that whooshed and splashed onto the deck. A thin line of smoke rose from one of the buildings on land. The people of Minamata were waking now, opening their blinds, and turning their faces to the morning light. Daisuke liked to imagine the countless kitchens, the bustle and busyness of morning, the people beginning their days.

They lifted the buoys into the boat and dragged in the long trailing net, before heaving the catch on-board. Takeshi and Daisuke worked in tandem like old dance partners, each long familiar with the other's movements. Takeshi held the net open, as Daisuke scooped out the fish and loaded them into the hold. A good haul today. The *shiroko* were tiny—no more than half an inch long. Back on shore, they would be washed, steamed and air-dried in the processing plant on the quay, then distributed throughout the country. Sometimes Daisuke liked to imagine where the fish would end up, his ambassadors to cities he had never visited. He pictured a stressed out salaryman in Osaka, or a pretty student sitting on a bar stool in Sapporo, eating the snack he had hauled from the sea with his hands. 'What delicious fish!' they would say, or in Daisuke's more lucid moments, 'These fish were surely caught by a wonderful fisherman!'

Back on the dock, he turned to Takeshi. 'About tomorrow, you're sure you'll manage okay?'

Takeshi nodded. 'No problem.'

'I could always postpone,' said Daisuke. 'Maybe next month would be a better time...'

Takeshi shrugged. 'What's different about next month?'

Daisuke thought about this. His work routine was unlikely to change next month, or next year for that matter. There was never an ideal time to take a holiday. Hiroshi had said the same thing to him on the phone when he had invited him.

'Okay,' said Daisuke. 'I'll be back Sunday evening. See you here first thing Monday.'

The next morning, Daisuke woke before his alarm, got dressed, grabbed the overnight bag he had packed the night before and let himself out of the house. It felt strange to be walking towards the train station, in the opposite direction from the sea. He had visited Hiroshi only once before, shortly after their mother died. She had needed a lot of care towards the end. Over the years, her eyesight diminished until she was blind, one of the many effects of the Minamata disease that plagued her. She always refused to call it by that name throughout the years their legal case dragged on.

'How can they name it a disease,' she said, 'when it was a poisoning?'

Daisuke looked out the window at the scenery passing by as the *shinkansen* hummed along the track. Small houses and fields gave way to high-rises, car parks, and billboards and then back to small houses and fields again as they sped through a succession of towns. His aunt should be arriving at his house about now to bring his father lunch. She had insisted on Daisuke making the trip.

'It will do you good,' she said. 'Don't worry about your dad. I'll take good care of him.'

Hiroshi met him at the station and they walked the short distance to his apartment in Ginza. His brother wasn't the same in Tokyo, far from the salty air and the sound of waves. His accent sounded different somehow. His smile looked like that of another man. Even his walk didn't look the same. Hiroshi was tied up with work for the rest of the day and had to head back to his office. He was the vice-president of some company that did something with computers Daisuke didn't really grasp the specifics of.

He had moved to a bigger place since the last time Daisuke visited, a penthouse apartment.

'Make yourself at home,' Hiroshi said as he headed out the door, briefcase in hand. 'We can meet up later for a bite to eat and a drink.'

Daisuke tried to read a book, but found he couldn't concentrate. He looked out the window. The street below was busy but no street sounds filtered up to him. The apartment was silent apart from the faint hum of the refrigerator. He grabbed his coat and made his way downstairs. He spent the rest of the day walking around Tokyo with increasing feelings of unease until his feet ached and it was time to meet up with Hiroshi.

'How was your day?' Hiroshi asked.

'Great,' said Daisuke. 'Great.' He took a long swig of his beer.

'Where did you go?'

Daisuke realised he had no idea. 'Oh, you know. I walked around a bit.'

'No work tomorrow.' Hiroshi smiled as he stretched his arms over his head. 'I thought we could go fishing.'

Daisuke laughed. 'Fishing, in Tokyo? You're joking, right?'

'I know a place,' said Hiroshi.

The next morning they set off early. Although on his day off, Hiroshi still looked business-like in a freshly ironed shirt and slacks. Daisuke looked uncertainly at the old sweatshirt and jeans he was wearing.

'Should I change?' he asked.

Hiroshi looked at his watch. 'We better get going,' he said.

They had to change trains three times and always run to catch the next one. They bumped into two of Hiroshi's work colleagues at one of the stations and Daisuke noticed how they bowed low and addressed him formally.

'My brother, the fisherman,' Hiroshi said, smiling as he introduced Daisuke. He replayed this scene to himself later. There was a trace of something in the way Hiroshi had said it — pride or scorn, he couldn't place which.

Ichigaya was both a train station and a carp fishing pond. They rented flimsy fishing rods from a little booth in the corner.

'Welcome!' chirped the tiny woman behind the counter. 'If you catch seven kilos of carp today, you get one free hour of fishing. There is a weighing scales beside each pond. Please return the fish to the special pool as quickly as possible after weighing it. Enjoy!'

Daisuke and Hiroshi sat on overturned yellow crates, surrounded by tall buildings as trains thundered past. They watched their two floats bobbing side by side on the green murky pond. Staring into the water, an image came to Daisuke.

He turned to Hiroshi. 'Hey, do you remember the bicycles?'

'The bicycles?'

'Yeah. It was around the time of the court case. They went missing and we found them in the sea. Someone had thrown them off the pier.'

Hiroshi frowned and looked into the pond as though the answer might be there.

'Do you not remember?'

'You have a better memory than me,' Hiroshi said at last.

What Daisuke remembered most from that time was the insidious silence. It crept up on them like goosebumps. By taking legal action against the corporation who ran the factory, theirs and the other families in the litigation group had broken an unwritten rule — putting their own needs before those of the community. In school, children would no longer play with them. One day when Daisuke was in the local shop with his mother, a woman refused to sell her rice.

'None left' she said curtly and turned to another customer. Their father found his fishing boat sabotaged, the paintwork scratched and the nets slashed.

'But things are better now,' said Hiroshi. 'The water...'

'Yes, things are fine,' said Daisuke. 'The bay is clean. Almost like it never happened.'

'And Dad? He must miss it since he retired. I've been meaning to get home. You know how it is.'

'Yeah, Dad is...' Daisuke felt pressure on his line.

'You've got one!'

Hiroshi set down his own rod and reached for the net as Daisuke reeled in the carp. It was small and muddy-brown with scratches on its scales, damage from countless hooks. As they carried the net over to the scales they looked at the fish, then at each other, and they both started to laugh. Somehow in this moment Hiroshi was his little brother again. Daisuke placed the fish in the pool and watched it dart back into the murk, aware that it was only a matter of time before it would be caught again. He wondered if Hiroshi had really forgotten about the bikes, or if he had chosen not to remember. That would be easier here. Perhaps if he was this far from the sea air, the boat, his childhood home and his family, he would choose to forget too.

Daisuke was relieved to get back to his routine on Monday. When they dropped off their haul at the processing plant, there was some extra mackerel and the manager offered it to Daisuke and Takeshi.

'I love mackerel but I'm not much of a cook,' said Takeshi. 'You go ahead.'

'Well, why don't you come back to my place and I'll cook it for us both?' Daisuke was surprised to hear himself say. 'I never cook just for myself and my dad doesn't eat fish any more.'

His father was watching television, a cigarette in hand, when Daisuke let himself into the house.

'Dad, I'd like you to meet Takeshi. He works with me on the boat.'

'Ah, yes. In Tokyo.' His father greeted Takeshi and bowed.

'No, not in Tokyo, Dad. He works with me here.'

His father frowned. 'Ah, yes. Of course.'

'I'm gonna cook us some dinner. I'll call you when it's ready.'

On the way to the kitchen, they passed the family *butsudan* and Daisuke noticed the fresh flowers beside the photograph of his mother. His aunt must have put them there over the weekend.

'Is this your mother?' asked Takeshi.

'Yes, she was sick for a long time.'

Takeshi nodded. 'My grandmother too. Towards the end it was...
difficult.'

'I didn't realise,' said Daisuke, an unspoken understanding passing
between them.

In the kitchen he mixed sake, soy sauce and grated ginger together,
then cut the mackerel into pieces and tossed it in the marinade.

'I'll just leave that to soak for a bit before I fry it.'

He handed Takeshi a beer and placed some rice and water in the
rice cooker. He turned on the radio and a cheesy pop tune came on.
Takeshi started to sing along in a girlish voice, his tough guy image in
tatters as Daisuke laughed and joined in.

Daisuke placed the food on the table and sat down with his father and
Takeshi.

'Looks great,' said Takeshi, helping himself to some of the mackerel.

'Dad, I know you don't like this so there's some chicken there for
you instead,' said Daisuke.

His father peered at the fish. 'What is it?'

'Mackerel.'

'Yes, of course. My favourite.' His father reached for a piece and
took a bite. 'It's good,' he said, smiling in turn at Daisuke then Takeshi.
'Just like your mother used to make.'

COME ON IN

They say the devil can't enter unless you invite him in. And that's just what you did, isn't it? You flung open the front door. Said, 'Ah, howaya devil? Come on in, why don't ya?' Led him by the elbow into the good room. Ignored the sulphur trail he left on the carpet. Sat him in the comfy chair by the fire. Told him to put up his feet. 'Good man yourself.' Take a load off his filthy hooves.

Your mam tells people her daughter fell in with a bad crowd. Too trusting, God love her — easily led. But they didn't lead you anywhere, did they? You sought them out. You ran towards them with abandon, arms flung wide open. Like the bicycle you cycled down the steep hill by the train tracks on a dare, because you were braver than your brother Eamon or any of his snot-nosed friends. Pedalling towards the abyss, the bicycle gaining momentum until that moment of free-fall, delicious and excruciating — An inhalation — then time suspended... them all waiting for you to fly over the handlebars... but you didn't. At the bottom of the hill you exhaled and the world resumed its spinning and in that moment you knew that nothing could ever touch you.

You saw him in Dún Laoghaire yesterday when you were leaving the clinic. When he saw you coming he crossed the road. You wanted to call after him. It's different this time, Eamon. I'm off it for good. Tell Mam... tell her... But instead you spat a curse on the ground.

There was no mythic pusher to lead you astray. You hunted it. Setting off like Shackleton into the Antarctic. Why? Because it was there. Because you could. And it filled the gaps, didn't it? You grabbed it like it was a life buoy that would save you. And you wore it. Yes, you dressed yourself in that stinking thing. Wrapped it around you until it became your flesh.

The keys in your hand are useless. She must have changed the locks after last time, but around the back you find the window open. With a dull thud you land on the linoleum floor. The kitchen is familiar but different somehow. Smaller, grainier. Like you're watching it on telly. You know without looking that the cutlery drawer is full of plastic spoons. You make your way upstairs.

You enter the pawn shop without hesitation. No invitation needed. Hand in pocket, the metal is cold against your clammy skin. As you stand twitching in line, your foot tapping an uneven rhythm, an image floats up. Sitting on the high double bed, watching her getting ready. One of those rare nights he's bringing her out some place. Before he left. Her hair like a film star and the rings shining on her fingers. She dabs perfume behind her ears and turns to you and smiles.

'Here love, help me put on this necklace.' And with small hands you reach and fumble with the clasp.

CURSED SLEEP

A bright slice of light shone through the gap in Páidí's curtains. He counted eleven gongs as the church bells chimed and cursed himself for waking up late again. Since retiring, he had been having trouble sleeping. At night he lay in an exhausted kind of half-sleep, thinking *I'm sure to drop off soon,* as every tiny creaking night sound was a booming red silhouette behind his closed eyes.

He padded downstairs in his slippers. 'Delilah! Lucille!' he called, and they came bounding towards him. 'Morning, girls.' He opened the back-door and Delilah charged for it, skidding across the wood flooring. Lucille wagged her tail and peered up at him. 'Go on, out you go.' He had rescued them from the pound three years ago. When he reached to pat Lucille's head, she cringed as though expecting a clatter, an old reflex she seemed unable to escape.

Páidí put on the kettle and looked out the window. It was one of those fine spring days that hinted at the summer to come. He made himself a cup of tea, sat down at the kitchen counter and stifled a yawn. He didn't know what had him so tired. He'd had a couple of pints in

- 43 -

Murty's last night all right, but none more than usual.

John-Joe, the barman, had placed a pint in front of him, before wiping a dirty cloth along the polished wood of the bar and announcing out of nowhere, 'Do you know what lads, I'm thinking of getting myself a girlfriend.'

The regulars who had been watching the match highlights averted their attention from the small TV in the corner. Páidí waited for the laughter and the slagging to start, but they merely observed John-Joe with a kind of benign half-interest.

'Is that so, John-Joe?' said Ger.

John-Joe wasn't much to look at, thought Páidí, but he was young enough and maybe that was the way of it nowadays. Deciding was half the battle, and once a man set a mind on something, he could make it happen for himself. Páidí had always thought of affairs of the heart as being like the weather. It was something he had no control over. Still, if it happened to be sunny one day he'd be glad of it all the same. There had been a girl once. Even now, if he dived down, he could drag it up and resurrect her piece by piece the way he used to. The way her auburn hair ebbed about her pale face in the breeze. The small hand that he wanted to take in his own. But the effort would be greater now, the strain of dragging up a useless thing, a rust-covered relic. And if he did drag it up, there were the other pieces that went along with it: that unwelcome tight feeling in his chest, and an image of Tom Mahon, with his boxer's nose and cock-sure strut, who could take whatever he wanted in life and make it his.

'Have you fags, Páidí?' Ger asked. 'I'm off them. Just want the one, like.'

For as long as Páidí had known him, Ger had been off the fags. John-Joe said that what Ger was really off was buying his own, as smoking other people's was no bother to him. Páidí didn't mind. He was glad of the company. He nodded and grabbed his coat and the two men went out the back into what Murty Ryan called his beer garden, but was really a cramped yard with some overturned beer crates for seats, the staccato thrum of the leaky gutter, and the smell of the jacks wafting out to keep them company. They palmed their cigarettes with tips facing in, and took deep drags, exhaling smoke that rose up above their heads until it was swallowed into the cold, starless Galway night.

'Will you give us a song tonight, Páidí?' said Ger.

A few months back, Murty Ryan got a karaoke machine for the place on the cheap, but despite pressing each button on the remote, then pounding several buttons in unison with his fist, he could only get the words of the songs to come up in Chinese. The microphone lay on the bar where the men shot it occasional suspicious looks like it was some peculiar sea creature taking on the form of a microphone to trick them, that at any moment would unravel its slimy tentacles and pounce. And then somehow after a few pints, Páidí found himself belting out an auld Tom Jones song.

His voice filled the dank corners and shook the cobwebs. Well, the lads looked at him a bit different after that and anyone who wasn't there that night and didn't witness it with their own eyes couldn't quite believe their ears. *Didn't know you had it in you, Páidí... Jaysis, you're some dark horse, hah?* And for a good while afterwards, they were at him to sing again, but he only laughed it off and shook his head and drank his pint and though he wouldn't admit it aloud, he was relieved when the karaoke machine died a death and as a final farewell act, blew every fuse in the pub.

Páidí heard the dogs scratching at the back door and he got up to let them in.

'Will we go for a walk, girls?'

The dogs began to bark as he picked up their leads and his car keys. He hadn't been out in the car since that quare thing happened last week and he realised he had been putting it off. He had found himself stopped at the front of a line of cars, looking up at the traffic lights, unable to grasp what they were. He watched a red light disappear and a green one appear. There was something in that but he didn't know what. Cars beeped behind him and he registered the noise in a detached way.

Delilah barked. He looked down to see his hand put the car in gear and it didn't feel like it was attached to his body.

When he pulled into his driveway later, shaking, he couldn't recall driving there. He wondered if this was how it started, old age and the mind playing tricks. When memory became murky and the past became the present or faded altogether. He should have told someone about it, the turn he'd had. He had thought about telling his sister Rita the previous Sunday, but when he tried to start, he couldn't think how to put a name on it.

She called up with a dinner for him most Sundays. She brought the two grand-kids with her last week and he had no idea what to be saying to them.

'How's school?' he asked and the young lad shrugged.

'Fine.' The little one looked up at him with dark, uncertain eyes like Lucille.

His sister ushered them towards the back door. 'Why don't ye go play with the dogs?'

The pair of them liked the dogs. They played with them in the garden, whooping as they threw the rubber ball for a frantic Delilah to chase, while Páidí and his sister made small talk in the kitchen. Páidí didn't trust the young lad. He was sly like his father. Páidí worried he might hurt the girls, so he got up every now and again and checked on them through the kitchen window with the pretence of getting a glass of water or the salt.

'Look at them there now. Having a grand old time,' he said to Rita.

Recently, Páidí had been finding it difficult to focus on conversations. Maybe it was to do with the trouble he'd been having sleeping. He saw mouths making the shapes of sounds but there was a disconnect between the sounds and his ear, or maybe it was between his ear and his brain. It reminded him of the baths he took as a boy on Sunday nights, the water tepid because Rita took her turn first and always stayed in too long. He used to lie back and put his ears under the water. Strumming his fingers on the side of the tub, he listened as the shuddering sounds filtered back to him, muffled or elongated, a strange yearning whale song. He was a deep-sea explorer in a submarine, sinking deeper than any human had dared to venture before, down into an ocean dark as night.

It occurred to Páidí that these visits from his sister were a scene from a play they had found themselves cast in, and every week they had to run through these same lines until all sense of reality had been eroded. What if he changed the lines, made up new ones? Improvisation, wasn't that what they called it? Instead of saying, 'You're very good to me,' when she handed him the dinner, he could say, 'Get out of it with your manky spuds' and fling the plate across the room. Just to see what would happen, like. Would she still sigh like a martyr and say her line, 'Sure it's no bother, I'm making it anyway'?

Sometimes he looked at Rita's face and tried to remember her as a girl. He knew that she used to tell him ghost stories that put the fear of God in him. One night, he heard a banshee wailing below his window and he wet his bed in terror. He still remembered the relief he felt when he crawled into her bed and curled up beside the reassuring warmth of her, where he slept dreamless and safe. He couldn't equate those things with the woman sitting in front of him now and it left him with a vague feeling he didn't understand that was something close to shame.

Páidí took a deep breath and put the car in gear. He was relieved to find he felt fine behind the wheel. He hummed a tune as Delilah and Lucille stuck their heads out the open back windows, one on either side, their tails wagging. He parked in Salthill and they walked the coastal path by the Claddagh. When they reached the playing fields, he let the dogs off their leads to run free. Lucille stayed close by his side. He bent down to pat her on the head and when he looked up, he saw Delilah tearing off across the fields.

'Delilah!' Páidí called, as he saw her disappear through a gap in the wall that led to the pier. He ran after her, Lucille following behind, but Delilah was nowhere to be seen as he stood catching his breath by a large pile of empty lobster pots. Then he saw her further up along the pier. She was wagging her tail and barking as a swan hissed at her from the dark water. Páidí remembered then walking the pier as a boy with his father and the sweet tobacco smell of his pipe. They had stood together in the spot where Páidí now stood alone. He remembered asking his father where the river stopped and the sea began, and how come they didn't get all mixed up together. His father pointed to the place where the Corrib met the sea.

'They call it brackish water,' he said. 'It's neither fresh water nor salt water.'

The young Páidí nodded as though he understood, but wondered to himself how it could be both things and neither thing at the same time. He found himself thinking of that strange territory before waking that was not quite dreaming, but not quite not dreaming.

Then he saw Delilah, still barking, make a run for the pier's edge, and the past broke free from the present, but not before he could reach her. She jumped off the pier and landed with a splash in the water.

A little girl who was throwing bread to the swans pointed and screeched in delight. 'Doggie! Doggie!'

Páidí ran to the edge of the water. 'Delilah!' he shouted, but the dog was paddling further out now past where boats were moored. He wouldn't be able to grab her from the pier's edge. If she kept going further out of the bay, she could get sucked into the current of the river and dragged under. If he couldn't get her to swim back, he would have to go in. Kicking off his shoes, he unbuckled his belt. The small blonde head bobbed in the water as he ran along the edge of the harbour wall, following it.

'Delilah!' he shouted. A crowd began to gather at the edge of the water, as he kicked off his trousers and threw off his jumper, his shirt, his vest. Some people joined in his calls.

'Del-li-lah! De-li-lah!'

Hearing the commotion, more passers-by came over to gawp at the frantic man in his underpants and to point at Delilah in the water and add their voices to the shouts. Some foreign students joined in, Spanish or Italian maybe, bundled up in warm coats like lagging jackets. They cupped their hands over their mouths.

'Dee-lee-lah! Dee-lee-lah!'

And soon a crowd had gathered on the pier and there was a chorus of voices — *De-li-lah! Duh-lil-aaaaah! Doggie, here doggie doggie! Dee-lee-lah!* — and over the cacophony of laughter, and voices, and hand claps came Páidí's plaintive cry, because this was no joke to him. Delilah seemed to hear them and she began to swim towards the screeching throng. Páidí stepped down onto the deck of a moored boat. He leaned out and reached over the edge and wiggled his fingers. 'Here girl, come on girl!' But just as she was almost within reach, a duck landed behind Delilah and quacked. She turned and started to swim back the other way, out towards the quick-flowing river. And Páidí, in his underpants, was screaming now. He was poised to jump in and swim after Delilah when a firm hand clasped his arm.

'Wait,' said a deep voice and Páidí turned to see a tall figure who somehow commanded authority with the utterance of this one word. The man reached his fingers up to his lips and blew a hard, sharp whistle. Delilah's ears cocked and she turned around. The man moved from the crowd and waved the dog towards the stone steps that were built into the wall, before letting out another blast. The crowd fell silent and watched as Delilah paddled towards them. Close now, so close that Páidí had to stop himself from jumping in to grab her. Delilah ran up the steps and shook dark brackish water all over her rescuers. They laughed and some even began to applaud.

'Good man, Tom,' said someone to the man who had whistled.

'Ya big feckin' eejit,' said Páidí to Delilah, or maybe to himself, as he clipped her lead onto her collar and gripped it tight. It was only then that Páidí looked for the man to thank him. He was surrounded by people, laughing and talking about what had happened, strangers brought together by what they had witnessed. Páidí saw the man's boxer's nose and the way he swelled even larger with the pats on the back and the admiring glances from the crowd until nobody else seemed to exist. Páidí found himself scanning the crowd of faces, searching for a woman with auburn hair who was not there — realising with a start that she could not be there, not now — until the crowd drifted away and he was left alone on the pier, awakening from some horrible nightmare, and scrambling for his clothes in the cold breeze.

That night Páidí had no trouble falling asleep. He dreamt of the Claddagh where the bay had slowed the surging river and the water was all glassy and black and in the dream he was in the water with the swans and ducks and boats bobbing and in the dream he swam with Delilah and Lucille and their heads above water shone chestnut and gold in the sun and they all three travelled out and into the current and down into the stream past the coloured houses of the Long Walk bobbing past in green white grey and red and then out into the open sea and under they went the three of them without fear and they swam with seals that were friendly with wet noses like dogs and down deeper they went to dance with a lullaby of green seaweed streamers as impassive fish drifted by and down and deeper they went as lobsters crawled on the sea floor and down and down and down and deeper still they went as darkness surrounded Páidí and held him in its embrace.

THE WEIGHT OF MY WORDS

Bernadette was good with words, but not with numbers. Numbers were red, angry, blurred things. Words had different colours, textures, smells. Some words were musical notes on a scale. The word 'sunshine' was a G. The word 'wait' was a B, but only if called after someone, and carried on the breeze.

She loved the taste of new words. She savoured them, then wrapped them around her like a cloak, a lexical cocoon.

'No thank you,' she said, 'I've had sufficient,' or, 'That man is rather bilious.'

She read *Mallory Towers* and *The Famous Five* and said, 'Golly gosh' and 'Bravo!'

Her father was teaching her to play the piano and she used words to remember which notes to play. She remembered the notes for the right hand by saying, 'All Cows Eat Grass' and 'Every Good Boy Deserves Fruit.' The left hand was 'Good Boys Deserve Fruit Always' and 'FACE.' Her father's fingers were long, white, and slender. Bernadette loved watching them dance their well-practised steps over the keys. They plíed and pirouetted. She thought her own hands looked like a bunch of bananas, trundling along the notes, hitting the wrong ones, at the wrong time, in the wrong way. Her mother didn't play the piano. Didn't have the patience for it, she said. She had a big collection of records and showed Bernadette how to put them onto the turntable. When her mother wasn't there, Bernadette liked putting them on at the wrong speed. Voices became lethargic monsters wallowing in mud, or frantic birds chirping in trees.

One day, Bernadette decided to speak only in rhyming couplets. She sat at the dinner table with her family, eating her plate of stew.

Her older brother scanned the table. 'Where's the salt?'

Berndette shrugged her shoulders. 'I don't have the salt, It's not my fault.'

He scowled at her. 'Mu-um! She's still doing it. Make her stop.'

'My brother's name is Luke, his face looks like puke.'

'Bernadette, that's enough,' said her mother, 'eat your dinner the pair of you.'

Luke flashed Bernadette a triumphant grin. Their father was pouring himself some milk from the carton. He missed the glass and it flowed over the table.

'Fuck it!'

Bernadette and her brother looked at him and then at each other. They had never heard him curse before. They wanted to laugh, but something about the look on his face warned them not to.

Her mother fetched a cloth and mopped it up. 'It's fine, it's fine.'

They finished their meal in silence.

In the summer, her father took Bernadette and Luke to the beach. Nobody used the sheltered changing area, because it was covered in graffiti and smelled of wee. Instead, they spread their towels on the concrete walkway, facing the Poolbeg Power Station across Dublin Bay. Its twin red and white striped chimneys splurted grey cloud into the sky. The sea was petrol green and when the tide was fully in, it covered the sand, hiding it from view. The water lapped at the edges of the concrete, where it deposited tiny shells and pieces of seaweed. When the tide was out, a small beach was revealed, but the sand wasn't golden like on television. It was the drab colour of wet cement. It wasn't soft either, but made up of visible small pointy stones.

'That's all sand is,' said her father, 'pieces of rock worn down by the sea.'

Bernadette started to hear new words being whispered at home: Biopsy, Tumour, Chemotherapy.

Cancer was the most serious of words. She hadn't realised this at first. When people asked why her father was in hospital, she told them, 'He has cancer.' It made people inhale sharply and look at the ground. So Bernadette stopped saying it. 'He's not well,' she said.

When he came home after the first operation, her father had a bandage on his head, and he couldn't play the piano anymore. His hands didn't remember how and his words left him. He searched for them and sometimes it seemed they had returned. He was tasting them on his tongue, but then he shook his head and said nothing. Bernadette thought her father was like Samson. If they hadn't cut off his hair, things might be different.

She was sitting with him in the back garden the day he remembered that he smoked. They were both reading as they sat together in the sun. He was almost his old self, sipping from a can of beer, his bald head protected by a sunhat. Her mother fussed, propping him up with unnecessary cushions.

'Now, you're alright there.'

It wasn't a question, but it didn't sound like a statement either. Her father frowned.

'Something's missing,' he said, carefully enunciating the words.

'Another beer?'

He shook his head and nodded towards his right hand, where his two fingers gripped an invisible cigarette. Her mother sighed, relented, reacquainted the two long lost friends and went back into the house.

Bernadette watched her father carefully bring the cigarette to his lips. 'Is the book any good?'

He frowned. 'Good. It's good.'

He'd been reading the same page for almost an hour. Words confused him, so she decided not to speak. They sat together in the sun in silent camaraderie.

There was another operation before Christmas. Bernadette asked her mother if this one would fix her father, if he would be able to go back to work, take her swimming, play the piano again. Her mother shook her head and she knew not to ask any more questions.

On Christmas day, her father was wrapped in his green tartan dressing gown. He was always in his pyjamas by then. No need for clothes because he never went outside. His feet were swollen and wouldn't fit into his slippers. Bernadette could see the cold blue veins of his feet. They sat, as they had done every year before that, exchanging presents from beneath the Christmas tree.

'This one is from you to mum,' said Luke, handing his father one of the wrapped gifts. Bernadette and her brother had pooled their pocket money together to buy the gift so that their father would have something to give their mother. They chose a box of Belgian chocolates because Bernadette liked the shapes of the sea shells and seahorses.

Their father started to fumble with the wrapping paper, trying to open it. 'Oh… thank you.'

'No, no, it's *from* you,' said Bernadette.

Their mother stood up and took the present from him. She kissed him gently on the head, like a sleeping child. 'Thanks, love.'

Bernadette's father didn't die, wasn't dead. Nobody uttered those words. He passed away, departed, was at rest. Bernadette's mother called friends and family, one phone call after the other. 'Yes… Today at the hospital… I know… Thank you… Tomorrow, the removal, yes.'

After the mass, everyone filed past them and shook their hands and said, 'Sorry for your troubles.' Her mother and her brother wiped away tears and said, 'Thank you.' Bernadette accepted the handshakes wordlessly and wondered why she couldn't cry.

The house was full of people after the funeral and every spare countertop or flat surface was covererd with food brought by the mourners. There were sandwiches everywhere — sitting in tupperware containers, or piled neatly on plates and wrapped in clingfilm. Stacks of sandwiches. Square ones, triangular ones, ones with the crusts cut off. As though sympathy was expressed with stockpiles of food and they could eat their way through grief and replace it with indigestion. It seemed wrong to Bernadette for this silent house, this former sanctuary, to be so noisy. Talk wafted through the house with the cigarette smoke, invading every inch.

Bernadette sat in an armchair with her legs tucked under her. A woman with fuchsia lips smiled a gaping smile at her, 'He's playing the piano in heaven now, luvvie.'

She could see lipstick on the woman's teeth.

The woman took a bite of her egg sandwich, 'Terrible hard on the kiddies, isn't it?' she said to her friend in a stage whisper.

Her friend nodded in agreement and smiled at Bernadette. 'Will I get you a sandwich, love?'

Bernadette tried to reply, but no words would come out. The woman with the lipstick said something else, but Bernadette couldn't hear her. She looked at the woman's lips, gaping like a goldfish, but the sound of waves drowned out her voice. She tried to focus on the woman's mouth, to make out what she was saying, but now she couldn't see her.

Bernadette saw her father floating on his back in a crystal blue sea. The water was filled with unspoken words in the cursive scrawl of his handwriting. The words formed gentle waves and lapped the golden sand where Bernadette stood. She stepped back to stop her new funeral shoes from getting wet. Some of the words were deposited on the shore where they lay glinting in the sun. Bernadette squinted, trying to make out what they said, but couldn't.

The woman was still standing over her. 'Or a nice glass of orange?'

Bernadette managed to shake her head and finally the woman left her alone.

The words swirled inside Bernadette's head like dead leaves on a windy day. *That's all sand is...* They tried to leap from her tongue, but she swallowed them back. She wouldn't let them out. She would never let them out.

BLACK AND WHITE TOWN

He was warmer than Gogol's overcoat, the book I had opened. I relished turning every page, sinking deeper into him. Since we'd met, I no longer spent my days grappling with unruly words or my nights buried in text. Not having time to write made me feel uneasy at first, but I told myself that this was living. I'd found a love like I'd only read about and I was part of the world at last. This is what it was about then: two hearts beating side by side in the dark.

He told me he came from a town of books. When we stepped off the train I saw that he meant it. We walked together through winding streets cobbled with hardbacks. The church loomed above us in an imposing tower of stacked bibles. He pointed out his old school, a sturdy structure of textbooks. On the way to his parents' house, I glimpsed a dark laneway of Elroy novels. The town smelt like curling up by a turf fire on a wet day. It smelt like the yellowed pages of well-thumbed tomes. It smelt like home.

His parents were waiting for us, standing in front of their hardbacked-house, like the couple from that *American Gothic* painting minus the whimsy.

'We hear you're a writer,' said his mother. 'Books are the foundation of this town.'

'Yes, literally.' I said with an accidental snort.

They observed me coldly. 'And what is it exactly that you write?' asked his father.

'Short stories.'

They gave me a sympathetic look. 'Oh well,' said his father. 'Perhaps one day you'll write a novel.'

Later, we walked hand in hand up the tall hill at the back of his parents' house. We sat on the crisp white grass and surveyed the town below us. Birds flapped past with a rustle of paper wings and the air was filled with the sound of pages turning. The sun was setting, spilling the last of its light over printed pages, illuminating fine layers of dust on book covers here or there.

'I love it here,' I told him.

'I knew you would,' he said. 'I've been thinking about it a lot, how I belong here, how I need to come home.'

I nodded and tried to muster a smile. 'I understand.'

He took my hand in his. 'What I meant was that you could live here too. You know, my parents have a plot of land. We could build our own house and live here together.'

I imagined the life we would have there, the two of us in our cosy home of short story anthologies. Eventually it would be filled with the bookish spectacled children we would have together — little Flannery, Alice, and Raymond.

'We can build a house just like my parents' place,' he said. 'Hardbacks, classics...'

'And some short story collections,' I smiled.

'Oh no,' he said. 'Nobody uses short stories. They're too slight, too insubstantial.'

I let go of his hand and shook my head. 'This isn't going to work.'

I forced my feet to move away from him. I forced myself not to look back. But already I knew that distilled through time and ink, I could capture him there forever, and render him mine again: that broken heart beating in a black and white town.

HOW TO DISAPPEAR COMPLETELY

The sucky sweets didn't do shit. Her ears kept popping. Maybe her head would explode and shower the plane in pieces of skull, brain matter and bloody clumps of dyed-blonde hair. Maybe she needed more sweets. She shoved another two in her mouth. *This too shall pass. This too shall pass.* Mantra didn't do shit either. She looked out the window. *Breathe in, two three four. Out, two three four.* Dublin was long gone and the sky was filled with clouds, candyfloss pillows stretching across the sky, like something you could sink into and float away on. That was a calming thought. But those clouds were a trickery of solidity — water droplets and ice, scattering light. She would fall straight through them, plummeting downwards, grasping at air as the ground rose up to meet her. She pushed the thought from her mind. Opened another sweet. *Breathe in, two three four. Out, two three four.* The clouds were beautiful all the same. She smiled at them through the window. They grouped together then and formed giant wispy letters that spelled out the words FUCK YOU.

'Well, fugg you, too.' She gave them the finger and yanked down the plastic blind.

'Is everything okay?' chimed the air hostess in the aisle, a frown threatening to crack her smiling mask like a rogue weed bursting through a perfect lawn. She was gripping the drinks trolley tight, her knuckles white. Was it possible she knew?

'Grand. Jus' don't like the lug of thosh cloush.'

'I see.'

The air hostess gave her a look she had seen before. People could call you crazy in a million ways, all the while smiling. *A real character, isn't she?* People should be honest instead of dancing around it. She couldn't understand why people said *larger than life* when they meant *fat, obnoxious prick,* or described someone as *bubbly* when they meant *insufferable pain in the hole.*

'Would you like something from the drinks trolley?'

'Double whishkey.'

She spat the mouthful of sweets into a tissue and picked up the drink. The ice cubes made no clinking sound in the plastic glass and the whiskey sent a shooting pain to her back tooth. It mixed with the taste of blood in her mouth. She wiggled the tooth with her tongue. Loose, but still not loose enough to pull out.

When she arrived in Schönefeld Airport she expected to see a line of police officers, to feel a heavy hand on her shoulder. 'Come with us, miss.' The tendons in her legs were primed, ready to run, to kick, to jump through the window — whatever it took. But there was no one. The man at the desk gave her passport a quick glance, looked at her for a moment, then handed it back.

'Danke.'

The other passengers headed for the baggage carousel. She had no luggage apart from the small rucksack on her back. Outside the airport it was dark.

She took a train to Alexanderplatz and walked around the square. The metallic structure of the TV tower hovered above the city skyline like something alien. You could get a lift to the top and look down, but that was nothing special when you thought about it. All cities had some yoke you could climb up, a place where you could perch above the city playing God. Streets like snail paths, and people like targets. Nothing real at that height. She had made a random selection from the departures board in Dublin Airport: Berlin. It could easily have been some other city, some other tower. There was no way she was going up there.

She bought a bottle of beer from a kiosk and walked with no particular destination in mind. The buildings were covered in graffiti, bold scribbles in primary colours on every surface — the city, a colouring book owned by bored children doodling during class. She scanned the poster boards and telegraph poles out of habit — *MISSING: Female, 5'6", black hair, stocky...* but there was nothing. Stocky, for fuck sake. That was the medication, not her. But that was all finished with now.

Dublin was a city of the missing. Every other week, she spotted a new face on the posters that were everywhere: bus stops, lampposts, telegraph poles, and shop windows. These missing people were always smiling as if they didn't realise the gravity of the situation. Sometimes word would come in — the canal, the pier, the Liffey. *Did you hear they found your man who was missing?* Sometimes no word would come in and families and friends would continue to wait. Then the *Fresh Appeal For Information* posters went up, and the missing continued to smile the same out-of-date smiles, forever trapped in hairstyles and clothing of years past. To her, each poster seemed to make the same incredulous demand: how can a person just disappear? It was both terrifying and ridiculous. When these people should be at work, or walking the dog, or picking up the kids from school like always; how very careless of them to evaporate. She had seen the Dublin missing, but never imagined she would become one of them.

There were no missing posters in Berlin. The posters were for art exhibitions, club nights, or techno DJs. She had expected to feel the weight of history, but it was absent. Berlin was not a museum. It pulsated. There were people everywhere. Energy seeped through the buildings, through the cracks in the pavement, through the gutters. She felt it reverberate through her body, cradle her bruises, and calm her throbbing tooth as she paced the city streets.

All she had wanted in Dublin was to be invisible, but faces leered from every dark corner. She wondered if this was all women had to look forward to, every walk down a dark street a potential *Crimeline* re-enactment. That was why she had carried the knife, for self-protection. She never intended to use it, but it was too late for that now. It was difficult to drop it into the Liffey. She was clenching it so tight, it felt like letting go of a part of her hand. After it disappeared into the murk, she remembered a story she had heard about swimmers taking part in the Liffey Descent who were warned to swim only in the middle of the stinking flow, to avoid the rats from either bank jumping onto their backs.

Earlier that day, she had been out walking and found herself by the Guinness factory where it was all cobbled laneways, shadowy buildings with steam rising up, the air hanging heavy with fermenting hops, and horses and traps lined up to cart tourists around. She was walking past the line of horses when one stamped its foot and reared up its black head, and she saw the red flame of its eye. She started to run, convinced she could hear hooves thundering behind her, feel scorching breath on her neck. She ran down one street, then another. Finally, she slowed to a stop and steeled herself to turn around, only to be greeted by the sight of an empty street. Leaning against the wall to get back her breath, she saw that she was outside a pub. She decided she needed to sit down, just for a bit.

'I don't like the look of those horses,' she said to the barman as she ordered a whiskey.

He nodded in agreement. 'Shite everywhere,' he said. 'You know in Killarney they make them wear nappies. Not a bad idea, if you ask me.'

As she handed him the money, she saw that there were small white flecks of paint on her hands from where she had leaned on the wall. She wiped them on her jeans and looked around. There was a warm feeling and a friendly light. They were on her side, all of these people in the pub. So she introduced herself to everyone and started warning them about the horses.

'I quite like horses,' said an elderly man. 'Man's best friend.'

'No, that's dogs,' corrected his friend.

'Yes, dogs are nice too,' he nodded and supped his pint.

She pointed a warning finger at the two men. 'Some day the horses will rise up, cast off their saddles and wreak vengeance on all of our soft skulls.'

The barman came over and said, 'Is there someone we can call for you, love?'

'No, I'm fine,' she smiled. 'Sure, I've only had the one drink.'

As she passed Warschauer Strasse station, she saw two homeless men fighting. They stood amidst the shards of broken glass from a bottle of vodka one of them had dropped. One of the men glared at the bottle and shook his fist at it. The other spoke to the shards of glass, as though trying to coax them to meld back together. Then they turned on each other, fists clenched. They circled each other, snarling like dogs. She watched them as people flowed past, pretending not to see.

She went into a restaurant and sat by the window. The waitress brought her a menu and a glass of water. The couple at the table next to hers had a brown dog at their feet that kept barking. The woman took a tinfoil-wrapped package from her handbag, opened it and placed it on the table. She took some meat from it and fed it to the dog. The dog was quiet for a while as it ate. Then it stood up and started barking again. The man and woman tutted and made kissy faces at the dog like it was a child. It sat back down and licked its balls. The couple didn't talk to each other, only to the dog. The man took a phone call and angled his body away from the table. Some people thought that animals were easier to love than humans. Maybe they were right. She took off her glasses to read the menu. The food was cheap compared to Dublin prices, but she realised that all the money she had in the world was in her pocket. She closed the menu and stood up. The woman had her head bent, rubbing the dog's belly. The man was still talking on his phone. They didn't see her passing their table.

Outside, she opened the tinfoil package and ate some steak. She realised she had left her glasses on the table inside. Maybe that was for the best. The lights in the distance bled into each other in a pleasing way. From now on, she would look at what was in front of her, and nothing more.

It was coming back to her a little, that old feeling she had once.

In the garden of the hospital the tree holds up its branches and weeps and GOD GOD GOD drips from the branches and she sees everything Everything Everything is Yes and That light spilling through ombre leaves is more beautiful than anything Anything Impossible to put into words such a thing when the words don't exist And she sees that she needs nothing more Nothing at all It is all there in her already It was always there but now she can see it And she can't contain her rapture She is fizzing with it fizz FIZZ and she falls to her knees…

When they dragged her back inside, she started to cry. She wouldn't take the tablets so they held her down and injected her and she kicked out and screamed and fought but it was no good. Then when she woke up, the tree was just a tree and the walls were snot-green. The radiators gurgled, and the hours, the hours, the hours crawled by.

Doctor Shanahan had crows' nests in his nostrils and a belly that spilled over his belt. He coughed a little dry cough after each sentence like it was a full stop. He told her that she had to learn to control her impulses. He hit her leg below the kneecap and her foot flew up.

'This is what you're like,' he said. 'The head doesn't know what the body is doing. The medication will control this. That's why it's important to take it.'

She shouldn't have told him about the dreams, about the horses: hooves stomping up the smell of sulphur, blazing manes, snouts of flames and wild embers for eyes. She saw him scribbling something on his notepad.

Maybe she never would have gotten out of there at all if it wasn't for Jimmy. He told her that honesty was the worst policy.

'The trick is to *kowtow*,' he said. So she cleaned herself up and swallowed the tablets that emptied her thoughts and said 'yes doctor' and didn't argue or cry or fidget or pace. She bit back her words until her tongue bled and she sat in her seat and nodded and nodded like one of those toy dogs in the back of a car. Then, just like that, Dr. Shanahan said she could go back to her life. And later she saw Jimmy with a couple of his friends on Grafton Street. She was smiling as she moved towards him.

'Jimmy! Hey Jimmy,' she called. 'You're out too. That was some hole of a place, hah?' And he looked through her, then at his feet, and then away as he turned from her and his friend's voice drifted back to her ears. 'Who was that, Jim?' and Jimmy said, 'Nobody. Let's go.'

On a busy street, she passed a hair salon and thought about going in, then decided against it. She found a shop and bought a small nail scissors. In a public toilet, she took off her hat and looked in the small round mirror above the metallic sink. Her hair was a tangled mess and when she tried to run a comb through it, matted strands came off in her hands. She had dyed it back in Dublin in another public toilet in the Phoenix Park, trying to ignore the burning sensation on her scalp as she sat in the cubicle and waited for the peroxide to take effect. It had left her hair bright yellow at the roots, fading to an orange colour in the centre, a kind of khaki brown towards the ends, and her own black that had remained stubborn at the tips.

She took off her coat, took out the scissors and began to hack through the coarse, dry hair, dumping the miscoloured strands in the bin. A young woman came into the bathroom with her small daughter and the girl stopped, saucer-eyed and slack-mouthed.

'Entschuldigung,' muttered the girl's mother, avoiding eye contact as she ushered her daughter into the cubicle.

A pale girl with cropped blonde hair smiled back at her in the mirror. Her face looked even more different now. Since she had ditched the medication, her moon-face was deflating and her cheekbones were reappearing. Now, with shorter hair, they were the first thing she noticed when she looked at herself, sharp as blades. She threw the scissors in the bin, then balled up her coat and threw that in too. It was a heavy wool coat that despite her efforts with soap and water retained a tiny blood stain on the sleeve. Probably not noticeable to anyone else, but she knew it was there and carrying it around was carrying the knowledge of what had happened and it made the coat even heavier. Being cold was preferable to carrying that weight, that reminder.

Outside, she felt light and new, like she could sing. Maybe people would mistake her for a German. 'Ja, nein, entschuldigung,' she repeated under her breath and the words were a comfort.

Ja...

Nein...

En.. Tschul... Di... Gung

Ja...

Nein...

They kept time with her footsteps as she continued to pace the city. Nobody gave her a second glance.

In Dublin, after she got out, she knew that they were watching her. The wrong skip in her step, the wrong way of answering a question, and they could bring her back in. She had heard things. There was a file on her now and a diagnosis and a prescription and a box that was ticked. There was no arguing with that. Her mistake was going into that pub that day and talking about the horses. Someone must have called someone because she was walking home when a car slowed and she saw Doctor Shanahan behind the wheel.

We'll just go somewhere quiet and have a little chat Nothing to be alarmed about so she's sitting in his car and he parks by the river She can smell the river and it's okay that his hand is on her knee because he's a doctor and he's trying to help her Remember what I told you about the brain not knowing what the body is doing? Yes Doctor You haven't been

*taking your medication have you? Yes Doctor Nod nod nod goes her head
They called the police in the bar Concerns for your safety You can see
that I'm fine you can tell them They'll listen to you His hand still on her
knee moves up her leg but it's okay because he's a doctor and he's trying
to help her I'm sure we can figure it out Cough And it can't be that he
means... here in his car His hand moving further and further up and she
sees that she was right about him About everything Yes she already knew
No comfort in the knowledge Just a sad recognition Easier to let it happen
Don't cry he says don't cry She nods She can disappear As he lumbers on
top of her She floats away This too shall pass this too shall pass... Out of
the car Over the bridge Down the Liffey Cough She opens her eyes Bushy
nostrils Slobbering mouth and every curse she bit back comes hurtling out
Calm down calm down calm down and he won't open the car Sits back
Fumbles with his fly Let me out let me out let me out Can't do that You're
a danger to yourself The knife is a warning Open the door Can't do that
Dull shock to her jaw He tries to grab the knife She holds on Her ribs crack
crack Stop Too late It sinks The blade then Blood His face Startled O His
mouth The blood Her hand Don't look she tells herself don't look She's out
and running running running into the dark...*

The Brandenburg Gate was all lit up. She had been walking for
hours when she stopped there. People congregated around, taking
photographs of the lady in her chariot, victorious on top of giant pillars,
her four stone horses forever in mid-gallop. She thought of the horses
in Dublin with tunnel vision imposed by blinkers, clomping on hard
concrete as cars zipped past. There was nothing for her to be frightened
of, she could see that now. It was the horses that were scared. Maybe at
night they dreamed of grassy meadows, far from the city and the river-
stink air. Maybe they dreamed of disappearing too.

Music spilled from the bars onto the street. People stood in
groups outside, smoking, chatting, laughing. Eventually, she would find
somewhere to sleep, but for now she was happy to continue pacing the
city, feeding off its energy. She needed nothing. She feared nothing.
Out of nowhere the tooth uprooted itself and came loose. It lay in her

mouth, cold as a marble. She spat it onto the ground.

'Good riddance!' she said and kicked it down the street. Piece by piece she would shed herself. Fade into the walls. Become the graffiti scrawls. Until nothing remained but a faded poster on a dreary Dublin street beside the Liffey. She would leave no trace.

ACKNOWLEDGEMENTS

Acknowledgements are due to the following journals who originally published some of these stories: *Chattahoochee Review, Writing4all:Best of 2009, Cuadrivio* and *Irish Independent*.

Thanks to: Nuala Ní Chonchúir for her generous time and support; Jack Harte, Clodagh Moynan, Celina Lucey, Seán O'Reilly and all at the Irish Writers' Centre; Sue Booth-Forbes at Anam Cara; Colm Devlin and Patsy Murphy for their teacherly encouragement; the MA in Writing programme at NUI, Galway: Professor Adrian Frazier and Dr John Kenny; Lisa Frank, Sarah Moore and Molly McLaughlin of Doire Press for their professional insights and input.

The Galway writers' crew for their help in workshopping some of these stories: Dara Ó Foghlú, Conor Montague, Colm Brady, Paul McMahon, Aideen Henry, Trish Holmes and Alan Caden; Andrew McEneff, my comrade in redrafting, for his invaluable feedback.

Special thanks to: John Murphy for everything; Catherine Robinson and Andrew Robinson; Fran, Tony and all the Murphy family; Maureen O' Connell; James McAuliffe; Benny Nolan for the road trip.

ABOUT THE AUTHOR

MÁIRE T. ROBINSON lives in Dublin City. She graduated from NUI, Galway in 2008 with a Masters in Writing. Since then, her short stories have been published in the *Irish Independent, Horizon Review, Crannóg, Cuadrivio* (in Spanish Translation), *Boyne Berries, Wordlegs, WOW! Anthology, Writing4all Anthology,* the *Chattahoochee Review* and *Telmetale Bloomnibus* (a Ulysses-inspired e-book produced by The Irish Writers' Centre). She was nominated for a Hennessy Literary Award in Emerging Fiction in 2012.